SUBMER

JOHN F. ALLEN

DV ENTERTAINMENT PICTURES

Based on the story and screenplay by Demetrius Witherspoon

SUBMERGE
ECHO 51
JOHN F. ALLEN

BASED ON THE SCREENPLAY BY DEMETRIUS WITHERSPOON

NOVELIZATION BY JOHN F. ALLEN

STORY BY DEMETRIUS WITHERSPOON & JOHN F. ALLEN

SCREENPLAY BY DEMETRIUS WITHERSPOON

BASED UPON CHARACTERS CREATED BY DEMETRIUS WITHERSPOON

PUBLISHED BY DV ENTERTAINMENT PICTURES
SUBMERGE: ECHO 51: The Official Movie Novelization

Cover artwork by Bart Willard

Print edition ISBN: 9781976099069

Published by DV ENTERTAINMENT PICTURES

First edition: September 2017

This is a work of fiction. Names, characters, places, and incidents either are used fictitiously, and any resemblance to actual persons, living or dead, business establishments, events, or locales is entirely coincidental.

CONTENTS

FOREWORD

Space adventure science fiction has a long tradition, from the exploits of Buck Rogers, who was created by Philip Francis Nowlan back in the 1920s, through E.E. "Doc" Smith's Lensmen and Edmond Hamilton's Captain Future adventures in the 1940s, and continuing later in the century with Gene Roddenberry's STAR TREK and George Lucas's STAR WARS taking us into the present day.

John F. Allen continues that tradition here in the 21st Century, using the worlds and characters created by Demetrius Witherspoon. Do you like fast-paced action supported by a narrative that moves like a race horse? You'll find it here in SUBMERGE ECHO 51. What about characters you identify with immediately whose success (and whose lives!) you root for from the first chapter?

That's here, too.

Witherspoon and Allen have created a future history that uses some familiar elements but bends them to their own purposes in this novel. The first character we meet, Captain Karman Tul, faces a dilemma that's immediately engaging, and then we're along for a wild ride. I read this in a single day, and was left wanting more.

It's clear that SUBMERGE ECHO 51 is meant to be the first of a series, and once you submerge yourself into this tale, you'll be waiting eagerly for the next installment!

Dave Creek

2017

Dave Creek is the author of the novels SOME DISTANT SHORE and CHANDA'S AWAKENING, as well as A CROWD OF STARS, which was the 2016 Imadjinn Award winner for best SF novel.
He's also published over thirty short stories in ANALOG SCIENCE FICTION and various anthologies.
You can keep up with his work at his website, www.davecreek.com, and on Facebook.

BOOK I

CHAPTER ONE

Captain Karman Tul dropped out of hyperspace to make his rounds along the outer edges of the Alpha Quadrant. Affixed to the display of his *Talon*-class fighter was a photograph of a woman. Her bright smile and sparkling violet eyes accentuated her unblemished emerald skin and spoke to their Veilosian heritage. Two long, black braids extended from the sides of her head to her breasts and framed her beautiful face.

He gazed lovingly at the image of his mate and longed to return from his tour of duty, so that he could embrace her once again. The imminent threat of a Krag invasion had the Global Defense Network on high alert. From the time of Tul's birth—over 100 years ago—the Krag Empire had been a major threat to not only Planet Echo, but the entire galaxy. In fact, it had been because of the Krag, the various nations of Echo formed the GDN as a planet wide military organization.

He'd entered the GDN Academy and worked his way through the ranks. Tul's hard work and dedication had been rewarded when he was hand selected by the Prime Minister to command the elite, Omega Squadron, whose responsibility was to maintain a line of defense for Echo.

"Omega Squad One to Echo Prime, do you copy?"

"Omega Squad One, this is General Luma, what's the report from the perimeter?" a sultry female voice replied.

Tul smirked at the sound of her voice. "All is quiet out here, for now. Have the ground troops been mobilized?"

"Affirmative, we have at least three battalions standing by at every major outpost around the planet. Also, the Dimensional Defense Grid is on standby, ready for activation," Luma said.

He nodded to himself and took in a deep breath to steel his nerves. The DDG had been in development for decades, but only in the past few years had production on it been hastened. The constantly looming threat of the Krag had every member planet of the Dimensional Alliance on guard. No one was safe.

Tul tapped a code into the comm and switched over to a private channel, which only Luma could hear in her headpiece.

"How are the children?" he asked.

There was a brief pause before Luma's reply. "They are doing well, I recently contacted their caretaker, Amandla. She assured me that they had been on their best behavior and every safety measure had been taken."

Tul pursed his lips and again nodded to himself. He had been away from his family for nearly three months since his squadron had been tapped for the border patrol mission. His heart ached due to the distance between them. He longed to hear the laughter of his children and to hold Luma in his arms.

"I promise to return on the next rotation if possible," Tul said.

He picked up on Luma's faint sigh before she spoke. "We understand the security you provide to our planet and to the Dimensional Alliance's mission. Yours is an invaluable service and we will remain faithful of your return."

Tul grinned. He knew that her measured tone was for the purpose of remaining professional in front of her subordinates. But he also knew that in a more intimate environment she would display a fiery passion particularly inherent in the women of their species.

"I appreciate your support, both you and the children. I promise to do all in my power to return to you safely," Tul said.

After a brief pause, "That is the most we can hope for Captain," Luma said. "Be safe."

Tul grinned. "Always."

CHAPTER TWO

Luma made her way back to the primary viewing screen of the Alliance Command Center and stood beside Lieutenant Nova. The tall, Echoian was from the planet's second most dominant of a number of humanoid species. Her dirty blond hair was pinned behind her head, with thin tendrils of hair—two on her right and one on her left—which draped her shoulders.

Her flesh was pale, even for her species, with white dots that outlined her eyes. The markings were common birthmarks for all Echoians.

Luma and her lieutenant had worked together for nearly thirty years and been friends for most of that time.

"So, how are things with Captain Tul?" Nova asked.

Luma fought to hide any display of emotion. "He and the squadron are doing well. As you heard, they had nothing to report on the frontier."

She could feel the weight of Nova's eyes upon her.

"I wasn't referring to the mission General," Nova said, with a grin.

Luma smirked in return. "I know. He asked about the children and how he missed them...us."

Nova nodded. "I suppose it's challenging to juggle a family and a military career, even under normal circumstances. But when the entire planet is being threatened and you're in command of its ground defenses, it would seem daunting to say the least."

Luma pursed her lips before sighing. "You have no idea."

Luma felt the presence of someone behind her and turned to see a young female cadet. "General Luma, Prime Minister Tungska has arrived."

She caught Nova's sidelong glance in her peripheral vision and ignored it. "Thanks Cadet, please see to it that our guests are comfortable and let them know that Lieutenant Nova and I will join them shortly," Luma said.

"Yes General," the cadet replied, before she turned and walked away.

"Did you have any idea that Tungska was coming here?" Nova asked.

Luma smirked. "No, but it's not surprising given the current events.

"Well, we mustn't keep the Prime Minister waiting," Nova said, as they made their way from the Command Center.

CHAPTER THREE

In a shimmer of iridescent light, three *Imperial*-class Krag cruisers appeared in the distance ahead of Tul. He'd never before seen technology like this in his forty-year military career. Tul had been briefed on the advancements in Krag tech, but this made hyperspace travel seem absurdly archaic.

The crustacean shaped design of the large, bulky ships gave them a menacing appearance. He knew that Krag cruisers usually contained a crew of fifty warriors, so this proved odd. Usually fighters were uses as scout ships, so the larger ships warranted his curiosity and concern.

He activated his cloaking mechanism and held his position to observe them further. Even Echo's most advanced military technology paled in comparison to the most basic of the Krag Empire.

The Krag Empire had conquered dozens of planets in their galactic reign of terror. They mined the planets for their natural resources and assimilated their most advanced technologies into their own. The inhabitants of the defeated worlds were taken as slaves or were harvested for bizarre experiments—called the Submerge Project—they had only recently become aware of.

He clenched his jaw and narrowed his gaze at the enemies before him. With over twenty years of experience as a fighter pilot with the GDN, he had trained for countless hours and survived plenty of dogfights with the Krag.

He grasped the control stick in his gloved hand and banked left in an effort to depart unseen. A soft ping from his instrument panel alerted him that he'd been detected by the Krag. A barrage of disruptor pulses pierced the dense inkiness of space and barely missed him.

"Omega Squadron report," Tul barked.

A gravelly female voice responded. "Omega Squad Two to Omega Squad One, I've got three Krag on my tail and coming in hot. Nothing I can't handle though."

Lieutenant Kharma Ping was one of Omega Squadron's most gifted pilots and an excellent unit leader. Despite the bravado of her words, Tul had known her long enough to pick up on the barely perceptible discord in her voice. A native of Sateria Provence, her lineage extended from a class of fierce warriors who placed bravery and loyalty as the defining measure of their culture.

"Don't get cocky Lieutenant. I've got three bogies on my tail also. These are most likely just scout ships. I'll alert Echo Prime. Don't do anything stupid until reinforcements arrive," Tul said.

"Me, do something stupid? Surely you jest," Lieutenant Ping replied, with a smirk in her voice.

"Omega Squad One to Echo Prime, the Krag have arrived. Launch the global defense grid and prepare the ground troop battalions," Tul said.

CHAPTER FOUR

Luma entered the large conference room behind Nova. They found a tall, bald, dark complexioned man and a short, red complexioned young woman standing near a long table.

The man was Prime Minister Tungska, leader of the Dimensional Alliance Assembly. He wore a scowl on his face as he stared at Luma and Nova. Global protocols were put into place so that Tungska was supposed to be off-planet during this time. The fact that these were being openly ignored piqued Luma's interest a great deal.

"Prime Minister," Luma said, as she extended her hand.

Tungska took it into his grasp and gave it a tight, hard shake, "General."

He nodded at Nova, who stood at parade-rest behind Luma.

"Leave us," he barked at the two men in his security detail.

The massive duo nodded and left the room in silence.

Luma gestured to Tungska to sit at the conference table. He sat with reluctance and the young woman followed suit.

"General, we've come upon intelligence concerning the Krag that is paramount to our defense. This is Kahmela Sol, one of the brightest engineers working for the DAA."

Luma eyed Kahmela and gave her a nod and wan smile. The woman looked extremely young for such a coveted position within the DAA. Due to the long lived nature of her species, Luma was often very critical of younger people. She wondered what this woman-child could possibly have to contribute.

"General Luma, as you know the Krag have developed advanced, trans-dimensional warp technology," Tungska said.

Luma pursed her lips. "I'd heard that they had some secret weapon in their arsenal. Is there any *new* intelligence data to report?"

Tungska cast her a grim glance. "I'm afraid so and it's not good. Ms. Sol has developed an enhancement to the Dimensional Defense Grid, which might counter any dimensional breaches their technology creates."

Luma nodded. "Why do I get the feeling that what you just said should be great news, but there's a catch?"

Tungska gave Kahmela a sidelong glance, which Luma took as a signal for her to speak.

"As you know, the Krag Empire spreads across galaxies, let alone dimensions, and has access to vast resources. Recently, we learned that they have developed, or somehow obtained the technology, necessary to create artificial, trans-dimensional wormholes."

"That's impossible," Nova snapped, breaking her silence. "It's one thing to manipulate existing dimensional breaches, but something else altogether creating one from scratch."

Tungska gave Nova a menacing scowl. "I can assure you Lieutenant, that what Ms. Sol is telling you is *fact*. And I might add, we'd be foolhardy not to listen."

Luma nodded, and flashed a cautionary glance at Nova. "I agree. Please continue Ms. Sol."

Kahmela flashed a sheepish grin and tapped a button on the conference table console. A virtual monitor formed at the opposite end of the table. The image of a Krag *Galaxy*-class command ship appeared on the screen.

"Footage from a test of this technology, conducted in the Theta Sector, was attained by undercover agents. It depicts the capabilities of their technology and why it's more dangerous than we'd ever imagined," Kahmela said.

The Krag vessel made its way through the void and vanished in a flash of light. The camera panned to a distant star cluster and zoomed in to where the ship rematerialized.

Luma's eyes widened before she turned to see the amazed and chagrin filled expression on Nova's face. Bile churned in her stomach as she thought about the applications of this technology. She was no expert on space travel—let alone inter-dimensional travel—but, she did know that a wormhole entrance was fixed in space.

Kahmela gave her audience a grave glance before continuing. "This technology creates what is essentially a breach in the fabric of the time-space continuum, which allows travel between two fixed points in space. This technology appears to allow travel between any points in space the user chooses."

"But won't our defense grid keep the Krag from breaching Echo's atmosphere?" Nova asked.

Tungska cleared his throat. "Theoretically."

Luma's eyes widened. "Theoretically? What the hell does that mean?"

A moment of silence lingered in the room before Kahmela spoke. "You must understand General, that we don't have a working schematic of this Krag technology and this is the only evidence of existence known to us. Obviously, any countermeasures we devise have not been tested."

Luma ceded to the thoughtlessness of her response, with a nod. Normally, she was not prone to emotional responses, but with the fate of the entire planet at stake, not the least of which her children's lives, she digressed.

"So, the best we can do at this point is pray that your *theoretical* countermeasures are effective?" Nova said.

Tungska harrumphed and gave Kahmela a hard stare. The young woman averted her gaze from the audience. "There's more-"

A loud klaxon sounded before a frantic voice came over the inter-com. "Red alert! Red alert! All personnel to their stations. General Luma and Lieutenant Nova report to the Command Center immediately!"

A weight formed in the pit of Luma's stomach as she and Nova turned to race out of the room.

The young scientist reached out to Luma and grabbed her arm, "General, this is the only copy of my research in existence. The Krag have infiltrated our intelligence network somehow. They know about our technology to stop them and they're going to attempt to neutralize it at any cost. Please make sure that they *never* get their hands on it."

Luma looked into the pleading eyes of the young woman. In the short time they had been in each other's presence, her face appeared haggard and dark circles had formed under her eyes.

"Of course," Luma said, as she took the small data chip and inserted it into her gauntlet.

Khamela lowered her head and nodded. Luma placed a firm hand on her shoulder before she turned and left the room.

CHAPTER FIVE

General Luma stood pensively behind comm officer, Ensign Drax Pol. She glanced over to see Lieutenant Nova at her station monitoring transmissions from the Battalion leaders.

Luma liked Pol and considered him one of the brightest recruits to graduate the academy. Luma saw unlimited potential in him and had specifically requested him to be placed under her direct command.

An alert chimed on the comm console, accompanied by a flashing red light. "General, I've got an incoming transmission from Omega Squad One, priority level nine."

In a brief moment, Luma felt a surge of elation only to have it quickly morph into dread. "Send it through."

Her husband's baritone voice seemed both measured and anxious as he called for the global defense grid to be launched and the ground troop battalions to be readied.

A lump formed in Luma's throat and bile churned in her stomach as she made her way to the far left side of the console. She tapped in her command code which set off a droning siren throughout the entire compound.

"General," Tul said. The grave formality in his voice and address, using her rank, only confirmed her fears.

"Report, Captain," Luma intoned.

"Ma'am, I've got three Krag Cruisers in hot pursuit, and I've lost contact with my squadron. I believe these are merely a scouting party and that the first wave of the Krag Armada is imminent."

Luma weighed the grim tone in her mate's voice and caught a subtle hint of something else which no one but her would…fear. Captain Karman Tul was one of the bravest and most decorated fighter pilots in Echo's military history. Which caused her all the more alarm.

"Understood Captain, I'll dispatch the fleet and rally the ground troops for Code Red. In the meanwhile, do all you can to protect yourself," Luma said.

There was a three second pause which seemed to stretch out for an eternity before Tul responded, "Roger that General, Omega Protocol."

The transmission ended and the entire command center stood still. The droning of the sirens had shifted to the periphery of her mind, as Luma stared in silence at the blank viewscreen.

"Ma'am, what's *Omega Protocol?*" the Ensign asked.

"Nothing Ensign. Dispatch the fleet immediately," Luma said.

"Yes Ma'am," Ensign Pol said.

A huge knot had formed in the pit of Luma's stomach. There was no official, military procedure named Omega Protocol. Only she and Tul knew what it meant and what it meant was, *protect the children and prepare for the end.*

CHAPTER SIX

Tul barrel-rolled through the void with the trio of Krag fighters hot on his tail. Streaks of crimson light pulse from the foremost Krag cruiser's cannons chased Tul's fighter.

A debris field—called the Delvian Quarry—stretched several hundred kilometers ahead of him. It was composed of the remnants of an ancient planet whose legendary history had been taught at the academy.

Despite his appreciation for history, the most important aspect of the quarry was that it would provide excellent cover for him.

Krag cruisers were some of the most technologically advanced crafts known in the galaxy. But, with regard to maneuverability his *Talon-class* fighter would prove to be far superior.

Tul banked around a large asteroid and between two smaller ones with relative ease. The Krag cruisers continued to pursue him at a far lower and measured pace.

He took a deep breath, which gave way to a sigh of relief and a sly grin. Tul knew it would be another twenty minutes at least before reinforcements arrived. His only chance at survival was to lie low and evade the Krag cruisers for as long as possible.

A sharp chime alerted him that an incoming transmission had been sent from Commander Ping. The dense cover the quarry provided was the only thing keeping him from obliteration, but it also stifled communications.

Tul hoped that his first officer was able to elude her pursuers as he had. Given her piloting expertise, he wouldn't be surprised if she arrived shortly to rescue him.

"Captain Tul!"

His name was all he understood of the garbled transmission. It faded into a succession of clicks and white noise, peppered with the sound of loud explosions.

"Ping!" he shouted, fearing for his first officer's life.

Tul knew that he had to join his comrade or die trying, which meant he had to engage the Krag cruisers. It would be risky and take some time, but he had to try to take them out one at a time.

He slipped behind another asteroid and moved with it. Tul waited for another to drift close enough for him to stealthily slip between them. This continued until he was positioned behind one of the Krag ships.

Tul queued up his targeting sights and aimed at where he suspected the ship's power cells would be located. It would be contained in a small area beneath the fuselage. Although heavily shielded, any breach should cause a catastrophic power failure and leave the ship defenseless.

Perspiration coated his forehead as he took in a deep breath. If he failed to hit anywhere outside of the two-meter area, the Krag ship would only receive minor damage and he would expose his position.

Tul locked onto the enemy ship and fired. The pulse missiles hit their intended targets and in an instant, the Krag vessel was consumed in a wave of crackling energy before it powered down completely.

In the seconds between sighting the Krag ship and firing on it, Tul had lost sight of the other enemy spacecraft and knew that he was now at a distinct disadvantage. However, in his mind he'd at least evened the odds.

His thoughts were interrupted when his ship lurched forward and the other Krag ship had him in its crosshairs. As he turned to engage and at least go out in a blaze of glory, he saw another Talon-class fighter swing around an asteroid and fire on the Krag ship. He immediately joined the fray and in seconds, the enemy ship was destroyed.

"Did you miss me," Lieutenant Ping said.

A smirk formed in the corners of Tul's mouth, "It's about damn time."

CHAPTER SEVEN

Luma took a deep breath and rubbed the space between her eyes with her thumb and forefinger. The message from her mate had forced her to confront the inevitable, *war*.

She picked up the data chip Khamela Sol had entrusted her with. What might be the only known chink in the Krag Empire's armor was contained here. The throbbing ache in her temple intensified at the thought of it.

Luma inserted the chip into her gauntlet and uploaded the data directly to it, effectively erasing all traces of information from the source. She ejected the data chip and tossed it in the small, incineration unit next to her desk.

All traces of the greatest threat to her enemies were contained solely in the weapon attached to her forearm. No one would think to look for it in such a device.

She scanned her sparsely decorated, private chambers. It seemed even more empty than ever before. In the dark, Luma fought back the tears she refused to show in front of her crew. Her position didn't allow for the appearance of weakness before her subordinates. She had to remain strong and sure, even when she was far from it.

Luma reflected on her military career and how she and Tul had trained most of their lives for that end. They had dedicated themselves to protecting Echo from any threats, both terrestrial and alien. However, nothing could have truly prepared them for this.

An attack by the Krag had been anticipated for decades, which gave them far too small of a window to plan and launch a defense against so great of a *Super Power*.

She glanced at the framed image on her desk of her, Tul and their two children. They were all smiles, happy in the moment and relishing each other. That day was a brief respite from the very hectic and work consumed lives they lived. Her only regret was that there hadn't been more days like that one, and now there would never be any more to be had.

A chime at her door shook her from her reverie in haste. She cleared her throat and sat up straight in her chair, "Come in."

Lieutenant Nova entered her chambers with bottle in her hand. Luma recognized it as Progenian Ale. A reflexive grin spread across her face, and belied her current emotional distress.

"Permission to serve the General?" Nova asked.

Luma simply nodded toward the cabinetry along the right side of the room, where glassware was kept. She observed Nova's measured cadence, as she proceeded to take out two glasses and poured equal measures into each of them.

Nova turned towards Luma and sat one of the glasses in front of her. "Captain Tul is one of the bravest and most resourceful warriors Echo has ever produced. Present company not excluded."

Luma nodded in appreciation of her friend's words.

"If anyone can lead a hard fought victory against the Krag Empire, even in the face of insurmountable odds, it's you and Tul," Nova said, as she raised her glass.

Luma followed suit and both women took a pull from their glasses. The rich blue liquid burned her throat as she swallowed it down.

A loud siren sounded and a red light above her chamber door flashed. The droning voice boomed over the intercom system, "Red alert, red alert. All active personnel report to your stations immediately!"

Nova filled their glasses once again. They drained them completely before they headed out of the room in silence.

CHAPTER EIGHT

Captain Tul and Lieutenant Ping held their positions when they reached to the outer rim of Echo's space perimeter. They had been joined by Echo's fleet of seventy fighters, thirty cruisers and one mega-destroyer.

He knew that even having one hundred ships to defend the planet was of little advantage in facing the Krag Empire. Their technology was derived mostly from the reaping of worlds they had decimated in their path of destruction and conquest. By assimilating the most advanced technologies of planets from the far corners of the galaxy and other dimensions, they had created weapons undreamed of.

"Captain Tul," Ping's voice droned.

"Go ahead Lieutenant," Tul replied.

After a brief pause, Ping spoke, "I wanted to say that it's always been an honor to serve under your command. You are the finest warrior and bravest man I've ever known."

Tul flashed a grim grin, "I only do what must be done, no more than any of our people. As for you, I had planned on telling you earlier today, but now seems as good a time as ever. Congratulations, Commander Ping. Your field promotion is now official."

Ping chuckled.

Tul had been impressed with the young officer from their first meeting two years ago, when she was recruited to his squadron. He couldn't think of any other officer more deserving of a field promotion than Ping and no one else he'd rather have as his second in command. Unfortunately, there was little room for celebration, given the dire circumstances they now found themselves in.

"I'm honored sir," Ping said.

"You earned it kid. Besides, Commander Ping has a nice ring to it I think," Tul said.

The console of Tul's fighter flashed red in cadence with a shrill siren. He looked up at his viewport to see a large shimmer in the midst of a distant nebula. A swirling miasma of light and vapor formed as a gaggle of fighters emerged from the dark wormhole at its center.

"Omega Squad, advance and target that vortex. Light 'em up!" Tul ordered.

Echo fighters sped forward and fired their heaviest artillery at the aperture. In a blaze of pulse missiles, particle blasts and photon bursts, the Echo Fleet converged on the tear in space and destroyed the Krag fighters as they came through the portal.

Tul held back and watched with a swell of pride as his squad took out dozens of Krag fighters. He joined the fray and together, he and his squadron had destroyed the Krag ships which had emerged from the wormhole.

"Woohoo," Commander Ping exclaimed, "We did it Captain!"

A gregarious smile spread across Tul's face in the wake of their apparent victory. However, it was short lived when a flash of light in the distance caught his eye.

The wormhole irised open in a swirling nebula of iridescent colors once again, only this time the center spread about ten times larger than before.

"Don't worry Captain, we're ready for another round," Ping said.

Bile rose in Tul's throat, and his heart raced at the sight he beheld. The nose of a leviathan sized ship made its way through the tear in the time-space continuum. It was easily the largest vessel Tul had ever seen. If he'd had to guess, he imagined it was about half the size of a planetoid.

The imposing shape of the craft reminded him of the mythical Dragos—a race of reptilian monsters who supposedly once roamed Echo several trillion years ago. Tul marveled at the sight of what he could only assume was a Krag Empire mothership. Their existence was only known in conspiracy rumor, as any civilization who ever encountered them were annihilated.

"Omega Squad, advance and open fire," Tul ordered.

His fleet responded in a dizzying display of aerial assaults, consisting of pulse and particle weapons fire. The barrage of his armada appeared to have little to no effect on the foreboding behemoth.

"Captain, we're giving it everything we've got, but we haven't even put a scratch on this monstrosity," Ping said.

"Everyone keep pressing, we didn't come this far to give up now," Tul said, on an open channel.

The confidence in his voice belied the desperation and fear in his heart. He wasn't afraid of dying, but his fear was that they'd lose the fight and that the Krag Empire would succeed in destroying their planet, their people and his family.

The hulking ship stopped any movement and hung in space like a satellite. A shimmer of light enveloped the vessel and sent a wave of hazy energy out from it.

Tul felt the energy wash over him and his fighter as his craft and the others in the Echo Armada were left derelict and floating in space. Some of the ships in his command collided with each other in explosions with deadly consequence.

Communication had been disabled and only the heavily shielded back-up generators remained to power the life support. Tul took a deep breath and watched as the Krag vessel hovered in place like a giant Arachnoid Beast waiting in its nest of tendrils before deciding which of its rapped prey to feed on first.

From various places around the surface of the spacecraft, hundreds of small, insectoid shaped fighters emerged and flew at dizzying speeds owards the Echo Armada. In a haze of blaster cannons and pulse missiles, hey decimated all in their path.

Tul watched in horror as his people were slaughtered with callous efficiency. He glanced back at the photograph affixed to his fighter's console and smiled at the memories of his mate and their family. A wave of erenity coursed through him as he awaited his fate.

CHAPTER NINE

A surge of adrenaline coursed through her body as General Luma watched the view screen in horror. The crab shaped fighters of the Krag descended upon the city and unleashed carnage.

Pulse bursts pelted the city towers which caused tons of rubble to topple onto the streets and bury the people below. Krag warriors descended from hovering transport vessels on zip lines and fired particle rifles at the fleeing citizens.

Klaxons continued to blare throughout the Command Center speakers but failed to drown out their horrific screams transmitted from the live public feeds.

She steeled herself against the wave of nausea and raw emotion, as her people were massacred in the streets from the alien onslaught.

"This is General Luma. The city's defenses have fallen. All citizens, please evacuate to the nearest halopad."

A wave of compassion and anger washed over her as she watched Krag warriors descend from their battleships and fire advanced pulse rifles at any citizen in their wake. Despite the sound being muted, she could hear the implied screams as dozens of images flashed across the monitors of the Command Center.

The Krag were relentless in their slaughter of Echo's population and failed to discriminate as to who they killed, men women and children alike.

"Where are the ground troops and why haven't they been mobilized?" Luma asked.

Ensign Pol turned back towards Luma from his console, "Ma'am, the ground troops are dead. Reports say that groups of Krag warriors simply materialized from nowhere at every base across the planet and took us by surprise. Every major base has been compromised."

Luma felt a weight form in the pit of her stomach. Nausea coursed through her even as she found herself clenching her fists and gritting her teeth in rage. At no other single time in her life had she ever felt so helpless than at that moment.

A strong grip clamped down on her shoulder as she was spun around, "General, we have to evacuate."

Luma gave Lieutenant Nova a dumbfounded look before she nodded and followed her out of the already empty Command Center. Nova pulled on the body armor and helmet, before she armed herself with a pulse rifle. "General, we've lost all communications. All personnel have been evacuated. There's nothing more we can do. We have to get to the halopad!"

Luma snapped from her reverie as Nova thrust a blaster into her chest. "General, we have to go now!"

A thick, acrid haze filled the corridors which severely compromised visibility and made breathing difficult. The two women gasped for air. Luma tapped the side of her helmet to activate the faceplate at the same time as Nova. Sterile air filtered through her helmet and filled her straining lungs.

Two ominous figures stepped from the mists, which Luma instantly recognized as Krag soldiers. Luma noticed a triangular formation of laser sights had landed on the breastplate of Nova.

"Look out!" Luma yelled, as she shoved her friend away.

Luma returned fire and struck the soldier closest to them. A well placed spinning kick felled the second soldier, before she shot him. She then turned and made her way towards Nova.

Luma's eyes focused on Nova, who laid on her back, as her hand covered a gaping wound in her abdomen. Blood oozed from around her hand and dripped to the ground. Nova's eyes were glazed and a trickle of blood ran down the corner of her mouth as she spoke.

"Luma, you've got to go! I'll hold them off as long as I can," Nova said.

Luma heard the approaching sounds of heavy, footsteps.

Nova strained to sit up with her back against the wall. "It's been an honor. Now go…*GO!*"

A single tear snaked its way down her face as she gazed at her dying friend. They both saluted before Luma turned and ran down the opposite direction of the corridor.

CHAPTER TEN

A large, brooding figure stood in front of the viewport aboard the Krag mothership. His hands were clasped behind him and pinned down the large purple cloak spread across his broad shoulders. A metallic helmet shrouded his head and reflected the light from the surface of the planet on the other side of the glass barrier.

For the better part of a century, the Krag Empire had cut a swath across the galaxy to spread their presence to the far corners of the cosmos. Hundreds of planets had pledged their allegiance to the *Empire* or been summarily destroyed. Krag technology had eclipsed that of any other race in the known galaxy by far and their latest developments all but ensured their sovereignty to all life in this galaxy and beyond.

"Commander Korvask," an apprehensive voice intoned.

"What is it?" Korvask said, without turning around.

The reflection of the figure behind him became even more rigid as he spoke, "Sir, we have secured every major city on the planet and all the units of their air fleet have been destroyed."

Korvask turned his head ever so slightly, "That's all well and good Ensign, but what about the Alliance Command Center?"

"We are encountering heavy resistance there, Sir," the ensign stammered.

A surge of energy filled the room and caused the ensign to stumble. Before he could regain his composure, Korvask had closed the gap between them and grabbed the man around the neck with one hand. He held the ensign in midair as though he were weightless.

"It is of the utmost importance to the *Empire* that we secure their Command Center. It is there, which the only threat to our technology in the known galaxy is housed," Korvask said.

The ensign gurgled and gasped in his struggle to breathe. His body began to convulse from lack of air. The pale yellow skin of his face, had turned to a deep orange color, as his large red eyes bulged from their sockets.

"Secure the Command Center and find the data! Kill them all, every man, woman and child. There can be *no* survivors," Korvask said, before he flung the ensign to the ground.

CHAPTER ELEVEN

"Shadow! Shadow! Are you there?" Luma called.

The holographic outline of a young male face materialized and hovered above the communicator worn on Luma's right wrist.

"Mother, what's going on? We heard explosions," he said.

"Is Amandla with you?" Luma asked.

"No," Shadow replied. "She told us to gather our things and hide. But when I heard explosions I went to find her and she was gone."

Luma let out a breath she didn't realized she had been holding. The caretaker for her children was likely dead, and they were alone and vulnerable.

"Hurry, get your sister and get to the halopad, now! Use Protocol 5," Luma said.

The virtual image of Shadow's eyes held fast to hers as his voice trembled. "But, Mother...I can't do this. We're not going to make it are we?"

Luma took in a deep breath and squared herself. "Shadow listen to me. You can do this, and you will. You're a strong warrior, just like your father. We're all going to make it. But right now, I need you to go get your sister and get to the halopad. Just get there and wait for me, okay? I'm on my way."

CHAPTER TWELVE

"Shadow, is Mother coming?" Lyte asked.

Shadow's stomach tensed as he continued to shove clothes into a bag. "No, just hurry, Lyte. Get your things. Mother wants us to leave now!"

He felt the nervous energy emanate from his younger sibling and caught the terrified expression on her face in his peripheral vision.

"What's going on? Why isn't Mother coming with us? I'm scared," Lyte asked.

Shadow paused, "I'm sorry that you're afraid. But, there are some bad people on their way, and we have to get ready to go. I'm doing what Mother wants me to do. Do you trust me?"

Lyte stared at him with a pained expression. "Yes, I trust you, Shadow."

Shadow reached out and placed his hand on Lyte's shoulder. "Good, then get your bag, please. Hurry!"

Lyte reluctantly turned and ran into the other room. Shadow watched after her and felt the lump in his stomach grow and swallowed back the bile which rose in his throat. The words his mother had spoken to him burned in his mind.

.

CHAPTER THIRTEEN

Commander Korvask entered the Alliance Command Center and surveyed the aftermath of their assault. Armed with particle rifles, Krag warriors fanned out and looked for any and all salvageable tech and weapons. He narrowed his gaze at the prone figure on the floor ahead of him.

A large figure approached Korvask whom he recognized as Lukaar, his primary battalion leader. From their days as cadets, they had always been rivals. It only stood to reason that when Korvask was given full command of the invading fleet—by the Empress herself—he would challenge him at every turn.

"Korvask, my squadron has searched the entire compound and they've yet to locate General Luma," he sneered. "I suspect the Empress will not be pleased."

Korvask narrowed his gaze at Lukaar from behind his faceplate.

"It's a weighted burden for the head which bears the gilded helmet," Lukaar said.

"We all serve at the pleasure of the Empress. Do you think you and the warriors you lead would be any less culpable?" Korvask spat.

Lukaar chuckled. "Well, you are the chosen one, selected by the goddess herself. It is of you she expects the most and any failure at this juncture may prove perilous to your military career. With a strike of this magnitude, even keeping her bed warm won't spare you from her wrath."

Korvask snaked his arm out in a blur and grasped Lukaar by the throat. "I'd be careful about what you speak of if I were you. There are some slights which could assuredly cost you your life."

Lukaar squirmed in Korvask's clutches and clawed at his hand in a futile attempt to remove it.

With herculean strength befitting his rank, Korvask flung his rival into a wall several feet away. Lukaar went limp and slid to the floor in a jumbled heap.

"Let this be a lesson in knowing your place," Korvask said, as he turned away from Lukaar.

His instincts were highly tuned to his environment and with incredible speed, Korvask drew his cutlass from its sheath and faced his enemy.

A flurry of pulse charges made their way to Korvask, who deftly deflected each of them with his blade. Trained in the art of war from an early age, in multiple disciplines, he had a reputation known throughout the far reaches of the galaxy.

Lukaar had since gotten to his feet and took cover around a corner of the long corridor.

A female figure fired on Korvask as she made her way across the corridor where he stood and down another connecting one. He recognized the symbol on her sleeve as one designated to an officer in the Echo military.

"Find that woman and bring her to me," Korvask said, to the Krag warriors gathered behind him. They immediately made their way around him and down the corridor in pursuit of the woman.

Korvask felt the presence of Lukaar behind him and spun with inhuman reflexes to parry an attack. Their cutlasses were locked, both in perfect combative stances.

"You dare challenge me?" Korvask said.

Lukaar laughed. "No one else has the courage to do it and none other the ability to best serve the Empire."

In a flurry of strikes, the two combatants engaged in battle. Korvask used his superior strength to press his advantage. He parried a thrust from Lukaar and spun around and made a downward slash, which caught him in the neck.

Blood flowed from the Krag warrior's neck in purple rivulets as he pressed his free hand against the wound to slow it. Korvask pressed on and forced Lukaar to the ground.

"Your death has been a long time coming Lukaar," Korvask said, as he raised his cutlass to deliver a final death strike.

A piercing pain shot through Korvask's chest as he looked down and saw a fist protruding from it. The shock gripped him and he stood frozen in place. His blade fell to the ground and he to his knees. Korvask felt his body convulse as he slumped to the ground, turned his head and looked up to see a man standing above him. Blood dripped from the man's hand, whose expression was grim and made even more menacing with ice cold eyes.

Korvask looked to see Lukaar standing above him with a lecherous grin on his face.

"See you in hell Korvask," Lukaar said, as he stomped on Korvask's head and he faded to black.

CHAPTER FOURTEEN

Luma clutched the hand of her son, who held his young sister in tow, as they made their way through the dark woods.

In her peripheral vision she saw Krag warriors emerge from dimensional portals near their location. The heavily armed figures advanced upon them. She knew it would only be a matter of time before the Krag closed in on them.

Luma stopped them in a copse of trees and pulled a silver, metallic orb from a pouch on her belt. She placed it on the ground and pressed a small button on its side.

In a flash of light, the orb expanded to ten times its original size and vanished. "Quickly children, inside."

"Mother, where are you going?" Shadow asked.

Luma reached down and placed her hands firmly on Shadow's shoulders. Not prone to public displays of affection—she reached out and held him in a tight bear hug. The scent of her husband's personal fragrance caught her nose, which Shadow had no doubt been meddling in.

A trail of warm tears ran down her cheek as she held him out from her at arm's length. Luma gazed at him and saw Tul's face and eyes staring back at her. How could she tell her children that their father was gone from them forever, and she would soon follow?

"You have to remember what I told you before. You're a man now and you must protect your sister. I have faith in you both," Luma said.

She watched as a brave Shadow fought back tears and stood with a rigid determination in the face of their crisis. Lyte stared at her in silence with large violet eyes. Luma had never been more proud of her children aside from their birth.

Luma turned towards Lyte, took the gauntlet from her wrist and attached it to her daughter's. Once affixed, it flashed a blue light and adjusted to fit her smaller forearm perfectly. She then reached into her pocket and placed a similar one onto her own wrist. Luma then took a talisman from around her neck and gently placed it around Lyte's.

"Wear these always Lyte, *never* take them off," Luma said.

"But Mommy, why do you have to go?" Lyte asked, with tears in her eyes.

"You must be brave Lyte, and remember everything I've taught you," Luma said.

Lyte flung herself into Luma's arms and held her tight. Tears snaked down Luma's cheeks as she squeezed her daughter back. Luma whispered in her daughter's ear, "*Esserepus.*"

"Will we ever see you again?" Lyte asked.

Before she could answer, the footsteps of the Krag warriors grew closer.

Shadow reached his arms around Lyte and held her close. The sounds grew louder, as Luma stepped away from her children, reached into her pants pocket and pulled out another gauntlet, similar to the one she had given to Lyte. She affixed it to her left arm and pushed a button. The area where they stood blended in with the forest and the children were no longer visible.

Luma ran in the opposite direction in an effort to lead the Krag warriors away from their location.

CHAPTER FIFTEEN

Luma stopped running and gasped for air. Her lungs burned at the exertion as her temple throbbed. A surge of adrenaline coursed through her as she contemplated her next move.

She scanned the area around her and saw no immediate threats. A few deep breaths later, Luma punched in a code to her gauntlet which activated an energy shield and in her other hand raised her blaster.

Luma turned and awaited the inevitable attack from the encroaching warriors. Her mind raced over the events of the past few hours. She'd lost her husband, her best friend and her entire race was now on the verge of extinction at the hands of the Krag Empire.

When the warriors came into view and gotten close enough, Luma rounded the tree and fired her weapon. Her first shot pierced one of her enemies in the chest. A blast from another warrior was deflected by her energy shield as she darted between trees for cover whenever she could.

Luma moved with battle honed reflexes and used her energy shield and blaster in perfect harmony. She took out another warrior in her path with a shot to the head, as a blast bounced off of her shield and took out two more warriors.

She had found her second wind and engaged the Krag Warriors with a fury befitting her own warrior heritage. An animalistic frenzy took over her as she defeated each wave of warriors she faced.

A stray pulse round grazed her right shoulder and caused her to stumble backwards. A zealous warrior had taken the opportunity to fire on her exposed forearm from a different angle and hit her gauntlet.

Her energy shield fizzled and lost power, as another blast from the Krag warrior grazed her in the leg and caused her to fall. Luma struggled to pick herself up off the ground as she continued to fire her weapon at the Krag warrior.

In an instant, she saw the warrior's weapon as a pulse round hit her squarely in the chest. An immobilizing pain shot through her body as a bitter chill took hold.

Luma fell to her knees and knew that her death was imminent. She looked up into the sky as images of her life and family flashed before her eyes, Tul, Shadow and Lyte. Luma felt her life force ebb from her body.

In one final effort, she managed to scream, "Srom Silaropmet!"

before she faded to black.

CHAPTER SIXTEEN

The minutes stretched on for what seemed like hours. Lyte sat with her knees pulled up to her chest and head down. Her arms were wrapped tightly around her legs. She tried to keep from crying, but the overwhelming sadness overtook her and her body trembled with each breath.

Lyte felt Shadow sit down next to her and place his arm around her shoulders. She fought back the tears and forced herself to be silent.

"Shadow, is Mother coming back?"

Lyte looked up at her brother and locked eyes with him. Despite her age, she could tell that he was scared too. She searched for some small bit of hope.

Shadow sighed. "I'm sure she will. She's a warrior and she'd never abandon us."

"Why hasn't Father come back to meet us?" Lyte asked.

He averted his gaze and took a deep breath.

"Father had to fight to protect us out among the stars. There's a chance he'll be back, but right now he's busy."

Lyte frowned. She felt a lump form in her throat and in the back of her mind she knew that she'd never see her parents again.

Shadow drew her in for a hug and held her tight. For the first time, in a long time she felt safe. She wanted to stay there in her brother's arms forever.

"I'm going to step out and look for Mother," Shadow said.

Lyte gripped Shadow tightly. "No, you can't go!"

Shadow extended his arms and looked her in the eyes. He took in a deep breath and sighed. "I have to. Mother may need my help."

"But you can't leave me here alone," Lyte pleaded.

Shadow pursed his lips and stood. "You'll be safe here within the shield. Don't come out until I get back, okay?"

Tears ran down Lyte's face as she reluctantly nodded her head in ascent.

Lyte watched as Shadow turned and walked through the shield and seemed to disappear. She released a breath she didn't know she had been holding and for the first time in her young life, she was completely alone.

BOOK II

CHAPTER ONE

100 years later…

The remnants of a once bustling metropolis, was now the scene of dystopian horrors, which its long dead citizens could never have imagined. Gleaming monoliths and spectacular spires now stood as broken protrusions against a shadowy horizon of somber gray skies.

She scanned the area, as she foraged for salvageable equipment and tech. The improvised hazard suit was all that protected her from the residue of acid rains and radioactive maelstroms. The toxic storms swept over the entire planet at least four times each year.

In their wake, a mostly barren landscape remained. Broken structures covered in lichen, mold and fungus—which were once the height of modern technology in the galaxy—had been reduced to the jagged grave markers of a civilization lost.

The twin suns had begun to slide down the overcast sky, behind menacing, dark clouds. This was a signal to her that she should start her twenty-mile journey back to her den on foot.

Echo City had once been the largest and most vital community on the planet. Home to more than fifty million people, it had stood as the beacon of hope for the entire galaxy. The inhabitants lived mostly in peace and prosperity for centuries, before the Krag.

One hundred years ago, a global population of over five hundred billion souls were extinguished.

Only one soul remained.

Lyte was that survivor.

The fire of hatred for the Krag burned inside her as she made her way through the desolate, debris strewn streets. Over the decades, Lyte had mined a vast majority of the viable surface resources. These days she had to risk exploring the structurally, unstable subterranean pathways beneath the city for her bounty.

The servo motors in her hazard suit strained at the weight of her haul. The mechanisms augmented her physical strength by ten, but the power cells only held a twelve-hour charge. She was down to three remaining hours to make the twenty-mile hike. Normally, it would've taken her six hours had it not been for the hazard suit's enhancements.

Lyte scrambled along outcroppings of broken slabs of concrete and twisted metal reinforcements.

An oppressive cloud with flashes of lightning loomed above and was headed in her direction. Thunder boomed in the distance and echoed off the dilapidated structures which surrounded her.

She had expected a huge storm, but her calculations as to when it would hit had obviously been off. Now, she was in a race to reach the safety of her den with her bounty.

An hour had passed, and Lyte's heart raced as she moved as fast as her legs could carry her. The heads-up display in her helmet flashed warnings that her breathable, recycled air had been depleted and her power cells were failing. An unexpected detour around a pack of Zortosk Beasts had taken her an hour out of her way.

She chanced a backwards glance at the encroaching tempest and felt the weight of it bearing down upon her. Several miles in the distance, acid rain had begun to fall. Lyte was less than a mile from her den, which was located in a valley on the outskirts of what had once been Echo City.

The low level area had provided her a measure of protection against the storms and lessened the amount of damage they caused to her home. She had built an underground decontamination unit about a half mile from her den. It usually took at least an hour to safely rid her hazard suit and any salvaged equipment of harmful levels of radiation.

Lyte knew there wouldn't be enough time to decontaminate her suit and her haul, then make it back to her den. It came down to her sacrificing a hard day's labor and much needed equipment, or taking the risk that she'd make it back to her den before the storm reached her.

She lifted a large boulder from atop a pile and revealed a metal hatch. Lyte tapped in a code on the keypad built into it and seconds later the hatch opened. She placed the equipment into the bin inside and sealed the door.

Lyte opened the cap on the bottle and poured its contents all over the hazard suit. The decontamination fluid would make it safe for her to remove the suit, but also destroy its circuitry. However, it was of little consequence as it would be destroyed in the acid rain which was less than a quarter mile and closing fast.

Her fingers worked feverishly to unfasten and remove the suit. The air singed her nostrils when she removed the helmet and caused her throat to burn. She gagged and breathed hard, but continued to unburden herself of the hazard suit.

A glance behind her told her all she needed to know. Whether she lived or died would be determined in a matter of minutes and she headed toward her den in a sprint.

"*Damn it,*" she thought, as she closed the gap between the storm and the safety of her home.

Running downhill helped to move her forward, but also increased her risk of falling. One unsure step and she could easily twist her ankle. An injury like that would ensure that she suffer a horrific death with absolute certainty.

She felt the first of the tiny raindrops against the exposed flesh of her hands and face. It reminded her of the sensation from a hot shower, but she knew that prolonged exposure would melt away her flesh almost instantly.

The drops which had hit her under-armor caused the areas to smoke and smolder, a precursor of what would come. Lyte stole a glance over her shoulder and could see the steady rain sweeping over the trees at the top of the hill. She knew in a matter of seconds that the downpour would catch up to her.

Lyte tapped a code on the gauntlet she wore, which unlocked her front door. She reached the door as a sheet of acid rain fell behind her. With only a fraction of a second remaining, she closed the door behind her and typed in a code on the keypad next to it, which activated the low-level force field around her den.

She fought hard not to pass out as she gasped at the non-toxic air in her home. Lyte turned her back to the door and slid down to the floor on wobbly legs. Her body shivered, her eyes watered, then she began to cry and laugh.

Every day was survival, she thought.

CHAPTER TWO

Two months had passed.

Lyte's emergency provisions held for the duration of the storm and the minimum time for the atmosphere to regulate itself within a safe level of radioactivity. She had rigged some of the weather control technology to help keep the area near her den safe from lasting irreparable damage.

The sinister clouds which had nearly killed her, had long since dissipated. The bright blue sky was a rare treat and one she intended to take full advantage of. The skies were mostly dim and overcast throughout the year, but every so often after a major storm, they returned to their former glory.

A grove of trees behind her den had survived the storm's fury and reacted appropriately to the restoration of Echo's atmosphere. It proved to be a perfect day to forage for herbs and enjoy the fresh air. Lyte strapped on her bag and headed out of her den for the first time in what seemed like forever.

Her strong, nimble fingers plucked leaves from the Pawtra tree, careful to pick only those ripened enough for consumption. She gently placed them into the brown duffel bag around her torso so as not to bruise them. The leaves were one of the few stable food sources left after the mass destruction her world had suffered.

She waved away a Markle fly which buzzed around her head, and closed her eyes. A gentle breeze swept through the edge of the forest where she stood. The warmth of the air enveloped her body and comforted her.

A faint musty odor slowly seeped into her nostrils.

Lyte spun around and tuned her ears to listen for the source of her nasal intrusion. Her heightened senses reached out to detect the unseen threat. With reflexes honed from nearly a century in isolation and having faced numerous dangers, she moved to her left.

Lyte was all too familiar with the Zortosk. The hulking, dull green creature swung its massive arms at the space where she had just stood. It moved with a speed and stealth that belied its large frame.

She bent backwards and back-flipped out of harm's way. The monster's impact with the tree splintered it and sent shards of wood flying in a frenzy.

Lyte landed in a crouching position, her forearms extended in front of her in preparation for the oncoming attack. A surge of adrenaline coursed through her and heightened her already formidable prowess. Muscles honed from daily fights for life, tensed and contracted, ready for battle.

She tapped buttons on the device attached to her left arm, which projected an energy shield. The wrist guard was one of few pieces of working technology left after the *Krag Onslaught*.

The Zortosk turned and released a guttural growl. Ropes of viscous saliva formed in its gaping maw of jagged fangs. Its massively muscled body was covered in a chitinous exoskeleton, which gleamed in the sunlight. The creature beat its chest with inhuman rage. Razor sharp claws extended from the tips of its three fingers and gave it an even more menacing appearance. With bestial fury, it bent forward, howled and charged at her again.

"Not today, monster! Now you will be my dinner!" Lyte said, as she drew her particle blaster from its holster and fired.

The power and focus settings on the weapon created an energy pulse—which after several blasts concentrated in one area—punched a hole through its exoskeleton and into the heart of the beast. The lifeless husk fell to the ground before the animal could utter a sound.

Lyte drew her knife and leapt on top of the beast. With savage fury, she plunged the blade into its head between the plates of its armored skin. A spray of yellow, viscous blood coated her face and torso. Her mouth twisted into an evil grin at her triumph over the dead monster.

CHAPTER THREE

As the setting sun gave way to evening, Lyte used the remaining daylight to once again enter the forest and collect her weekly allotment of firewood. The Zortosk had been gutted and was ready for roasting.

The animal's exoskeleton would provide plates for the hazard suit, to replace the one she'd lost in the storm. When tempered in fire, the exoskeleton changed in color from a dull green to a dark brown. She took a moment and looked at the emerald green flesh of her hands. Lyte marveled that her race, and so hideous of a creature shared even the slightest bit of common ancestry.

Its flesh would provide her sustenance for the next few days and save her some time from her weekly hunt. A grim smirk eased across her face. The *Kill Frenzy* had been stronger than ever before. Her abilities had begun to expand, as she found it much easier to slay beasts that a mere twenty years ago, would've proven far more challenging.

Lyte had combed the data archives which had survived the onslaught and learned much about her physiology which her mother had not had the time to pass on to her. According to what she'd read, it was at her current age that she'd reach her peak.

There was so much that she'd wished that she could have learned from her mother, instead of data files. Every day since the day she'd lost her, Lyte longed for her mother's guidance and love. As a child, she had often wondered why her parents had taught her survival skills at such an early age. While other children were playing games and lived a carefree life, she and Shadow were learning to fight to live in a world that somehow they knew she'd end up living in.

Lyte stirred from her reverie when her ears perked at a faint whizzing sound.

She closed her eyes and determined that the noise was coming from above her. As she opened her eyes and looked to the sky, a group of meteors streaked down from the heavens.

Many of the smaller ones burned and disintegrated in midair, while other slightly larger ones, hit the side of a nearby mountain. Their impacts caused an explosion of rocks. A minor landslide erupted and in its center was a flash of blue light and electricity.

Lyte dropped the wood she had collected and sprinted toward the mountain to investigate.

CHAPTER FOUR

After an hour long climb, Lyte reached the area on the mountainside where she saw the flash of light. Besides the obvious disturbance of rocks, nothing seemed too out of place at first glance.

She took each step with care, as the mountain area was treacherous under normal circumstances, let alone after a meteor impact and resulting rockslide. As she made her way farther along the mountainside, she spotted a gray, metallic pod imbedded in the rocks. It appeared to have suffered damage from its collision with the mountain. Blue bolts of electrical energy shrouded the ovoid structure.

Lyte approached the pod, stepping lightly and with her blaster drawn. As she drew closer, she recognized it to be a Stasis Pod. Lyte used her free hand to wipe the condensation from the front of the glass window on the pod. She peered inside and saw a humanoid male. A patch stitched to the upper left breast area of his jumpsuit contained the number 51.

In an instant, the man's eyes popped open and Lyte jumped back in surprise. She aimed her weapon at the pod and took several steps backwards.

The man's eyes closed.

Lyte scanned the area for anything or anyone else. She soon came to the conclusion that he had been alone. The setting sun glinted light off a piece of metal on the ground a few meters away. She walked to it, picked it up and after examining it, clipped it to her clothes.

She managed to open the stasis pod with a well-placed shot from her blaster and a nearby, heavy stone.

CHAPTER FIVE

The last remnants of day were fading fast when Lyte reached her den. It had taken considerable effort to get the man down the side of the mountain and through the forest.

She didn't think she'd make it back before dark given that she had to climb back down the mountain to get rope and a few other supplies, then climb back up to retrieve the stranger.

Lyte secured the cyborg to the door of the pod, which she used as a makeshift transport. She had to fit gravity dampeners to the apparatus and use a portable pulley, she embedded into the side of the mountain, to lower him.

She then dragged him to her den and went back out to re-gather the firewood she had collected earlier. Lyte set the man inside, placed some of the wood into the fireplace and started a fire there. She then used the remainder to start a fire under the Zortosk Beast, so that it could start roasting.

Lyte ran a portable medical scanner over the man's body and determined that he wasn't entirely human. Cybernetic implants had replaced or enhanced all of his internal organs with mechanical and computerized systems. Nanites in his exterior pseudo-flesh kept the organic parts alive.

Lyte removed the cyborg from the improvised transport and sat him in a chair. She used the rope to secure him to the chair as tightly as possible, then gathered and spread out various tools onto her dining table.

She noticed a protrusion in the back of his head and wanted to examine it further. The circuitry was extremely advanced and she wasn't entirely certain she'd be able to make the necessary repairs.

Lyte accessed the data files on cyborg circuitry in her gauntlet and determined that the data chip had been damaged. After a rudimentary scan of his cybernetic enhanced brain and its central processing matrix assembly, she found the damaged data chip and began to remove it.

Before she could act, the cyborg's eyes opened and its body stiffened. It stared straight ahead and began to repeat, "Echo 51, Echo 51, Echo 51."

"Oh damn," she said.

Lyte immediately attempted to access the data on how to shut down the cybernetic subroutines in his brain.

"There's got to be a way to shut this thing down," she said.

When all technological means failed, she relied upon the tried and true physical method of blunt force impact.

She balled her right fist, cupped it with her left hand, then raised her arms over her head. With every last reserve of strength, she could muster, she brought her hands down against the back of the cyborg's head.

A flash of electricity preceded the cyborg's silence. Lyte rechecked the ropes, and after deciding that they held secure, decided to attempt removing the damaged data chip once more.

After several more attempts, she succeeded in removing the damaged chip. She inserted it into a handheld data transfer device and transferred the data available, onto another data chip. Once the transfer was complete, she placed the *new* data chip into the cyborg's CPU.

The cyborg's eyelids began to flicker and his vocal processors started to sputter. Its eyes focused on Lyte as she stepped in front of it.

"Where am I?" the cyborg said.

Lyte stared at it and stood in a minimally defensive stance. She didn't want to appear threatening, but she also wanted to be ready for anything.

"You're okay. This is my den. Your pod was severely damaged from the meteor shower. What exactly are you? Are you from the far side of Echo?" Lyte asked.

The cyborg face twisted into an eerily human look of confusion. It seemed to be working hard at processing the questions and finding a response.

"I am a CG unit, class 51. I seem to be having difficulty accessing the files on my origin," the cyborg said, as it paused and stared with a blank expression.

Lyte walked around it and leaned in to look at the damaged area on its head. "Have you seen my species before?"

"I am unable to access my data files containing species classifications at this time," the cyborg replied.

A surge of impatience and frustration washed over Lyte at the cyborg's limited responses.

"Well, do you have a name?" she asked, as she stepped back in front of it.

The cyborg looked at her with a puzzled expression.

She gave him an irritated sigh and frowned, "Well, I'll call you *51* for now."

CHAPTER SIX

Lyte had prepared a meal for them before they started their chores for the day. She set down two plates on the table. One, she placed in front of her seat and the other in front of 51.

"You do eat food, don't you?" Lyte asked.

He looked up at her and smiled. The weight of his gaze captured her eyes. She felt something inside her which she'd never experienced before. A flood of emotions caused her to experience an intense attraction to 51 she couldn't explain. Heat rose from Lyte's face and her heart started beating faster than normal.

"Yes, I am able to assimilate organic substances for my energy reserves. What is this?" 51 asked.

Lyte sat down across from him. "Zarnian eggs, Kuukla Beast bellies and bread."

51 stared at her with a seductive grin on his face. "It smells…inviting."

Lyte averted her gaze with a sheepish smile. She'd never realized how 51's features were so pleasing to look at until now.

Lyte looked up again at 51. "Why are you staring at me like that?" she asked.

51 paused before he replied, "Your eyes are white. I noticed by accessing the data files for this planet that others of your species have brown eyes. Why are yours so different?"

Lyte frowned as she looked away. "I don't know. I can see things differently than others of my species. It is a genetic mutation which has never occurred within my race before."

51 nodded, "An intriguing evolutionary adaptation."

They ate in awkward silence. Every so often she'd lift her gaze, glance at 51 and catch him eyeing her with lecherous glare.

When they finished eating, she gathered the empty plates and took them to the sink for cleansing. She sensed his eyes on her, his gaze caused her heart to flutter and her breaths to become shallow.

"How can I assist you?" 51 asked.

She refused to turn around, as she responded. "It's alright, I've got it," she mumbled.

He stood close behind her and placed his hands on her hips. Her entire body tensed and began to shake. His lips grazed her ears gently as he whispered, "Are you certain?"

Lyte sat up in her bed and gasped for air. Beads of perspiration dotted her forehead and a chill shot through her body. She glanced over to the chair and immediately realized that 51 was gone.

She jumped up and quickly grabbed her weapons and strapped them on as she ran out the door.

CHAPTER SEVEN

Lyte ran towards the familiar animal sounds which reverberated through the forest. Her heart raced at the thought of what she might find.

Once she reached the clearing, she saw 51 facing a Zortosk Beast. The creature roared and dropped to the ground in an aggressive stance. It charged at 51, and narrowed the gap between them with inhuman speed. The beast rammed 51 head on, hit him squarely in the chest, and knocked him back into the woods.

The creature slowly stalked towards where 51 had been thrown. Lyte charged the Zortosk Beast.

"Come earn your meal. Come on beast!

The Zortosk swiped its massive arm in Lyte's direction and knocked her off her feet. It raised its foot over Lyte, who barely managed to roll out of the way.

She forced herself to her feet and reached for her blaster. With dizzying speed, the creature grabbed Lyte's arm and squeezed it with tremendous force.

Lyte dropped the blaster as the Zortosk used its other hand to grab her around the neck and pulled her towards its gaping maw. The foul stench of its breath sent a wave of nausea through her.

She focused her will and threw her head forward to head-butt the beast and stun it. The Zortosk loosened its grip on her and she raised her legs, planted her feet on its chest and pushed off.

Lyte flipped away from the beast, landed on her feet and fired her blaster at the creature. The rounds destroyed the beast's legs and it staggered into a tree and slid down to the ground.

She pulled out her long blade, and stalked toward the incapacitated creature. With three deft strikes, Lyte tore into the Zortosk's belly. She took a few seconds to make sure it was dead, and turned toward the forest to find 51. Lyte spotted him in a copse of trees and rushed over to him.

"51…51, can you hear me?" Lyte asked.

In the distance, the roar of other Zortosk Beasts rang out. Lyte, knew they couldn't remain there any longer, so she grabbed 51's arm and pulled him up. She struggled with his weight, but managed to get him up on his feet and place an arm around her neck. Lyte half supported, half

dragged him through the woods and back to her den.

CHAPTER EIGHT

Lyte placed 51 back into the chair and began to check the extent of his damage. She attempted to access some data files that might help, but none proved very useful.

"51…51, wake up!" she said.

51 remained inhumanly still and silence lingered for several seconds before his eyes began to flutter. In an instant, they popped open and fixated on Lyte.

"Lyte, are you hurt? Do you require medical attention?"

Lyte's pursed lips slid into a mild grin at the cyborg's awakening. She felt an odd urge to embrace him.

"No, but you do," Lyte said.

51 looked away and froze. He stared off into space for about five seconds before he turned back to Lyte. "There appears to be no major internal damage. The nanites in my flesh are working to rapidly heal any injuries my organic systems may have suffered. I should be completely

functional in less than an hour. Your health maintenance is likely much more critical than mine."

Lyte smiled at his response. "I'm fine," she said.

So far as she knew him, it was consistent with the cyborg's behavior to brush off any threats to himself, and focus his concern on her. There had been no one since her family was killed, to care about her. She was unaccustomed to this level of care, which caused her to experience gratitude and joy, while still feeling uncomfortable.

"I think the chores can wait a couple of hours, while we both get a bit of rest. Perhaps you should switch to, 'Standby Mode' while you run a complete diagnostic?" Lyte said.

51 nodded, sat rigid in the chair and faced forward with a blank stare. Lyte reflected on how good it felt not to be alone anymore. The decades of isolation had taken their toll and at times caused her to reevaluate her purpose.

She made her way to her bedchamber and lowered herself down onto her bed. Her entire body ached, so she made every effort to remain completely still, despite her mind racing a mile a minute.

After a minute, she fell asleep. Her last thought was the possibility of finishing her dream.

CHAPTER NINE

The midday sun made its best attempt to squeeze through the overcast sky, but failed as always. Lyte knew next to nothing about cybernetics, let alone those as advanced as 51's. It proved tedious and at times maddening to mine the fractured and eroded digital archives which remained after the *Onslaught*.

However, she worked with near inhuman stamina and determination to repair 51's damaged circuits.

"I would like to thank you for repairing my damaged implant," 51 said.

Lyte refused to acknowledge his gratitude and instead, chose to address her own concerns and frustrations which led to her current task.

"What were you doing out there all by yourself? The forest has many dangers. You must never leave this place without me," she said.

"I regret my actions. My biotronic core has been bothering me while in low power mode. The images are faint, but complex," 51 said.

Lyte gave him a quizzical look. "You mean while you were sleeping? Do you... dream, 51? How is that possible?"

"Dreams are not in my programming. Images may formulate in my positronic brain, giving me what you would call memories. However, these images tend to confuse me."

"What do you see?" Lyte asked.

51 stared ahead with an inhuman expression, devoid of any emotion. The silence lingered for several seconds before he spoke.

"I saw a large spacecraft. There was a power struggle and a great battle. Many died and an entire planet was devastated. Any other details are not clear," 51 said.

"It's okay, take your time," Lyte said, as she rested her hand on his shoulder.

The cyborg continued, "I saw a vast number of galaxies, planets, and living stars. They all have names. An armada of Starfighters and larger ships invading other planets. Two men locked in battle, a bloody fist and raucous laughter. Flashes of destruction followed, and then complete darkness, the vacuum of space. What does this mean to you Lyte? Are my implants beyond repairing? If so I do not want these memories, please delete them."

Lyte fixed him with a sympathetic gaze. "I don't know if that's even possible. I'll have to look into it."

"Thank you Lyte," 51 replied.

Lyte gave him a perplexed glance, "For what?"

51 cocked his head and paused before he spoke.

"You could have left me there, and my life mold would have been lost. Therefore, I am indebted to you," 51 said.

Lyte turned and moved away from him, towards the table. Her hands trembled as she began to replace her tools. A slight timbre of human emotion had been imbued in 51's words. For the briefest of moments, he reminded her of Shadow. Memories flashed through her mind of her lost brother. She'd always looked up to him and knew he'd have her back at any time. Lyte owed her life to him many times over. It was a debt, she could never have repaid and would never have the opportunity to do so.

"What else was I to do? There are things around here that need repair, so I drug you back here. I don't need your words of gratitude. What I need, is your commitment to stay out of danger and help me when I ask," she said.

51 stared blankly at her and nodded. "Then I will get started immediately."

He rose from his seat and left the den in silence.

CHAPTER TEN

Lyte marveled at 51's endless stamina. Within three hours, he had singlehandedly plowed the small vegetable grove behind her den, collected a week's supply of fruits, and gathered the night's firewood.

She sometimes found herself staring at how his synthetic muscles bulged with every labor he performed. His tanned skin was without blemish or fault and his hair neatly kempt. 51 stood about three meters tall and had a lithe, well-proportioned body. With each movement, the sleeves of his tunic glowed with power.

He wasn't nearly as tall and robust as she remembered her father to be, but nonetheless there was something aesthetically pleasing about him. Most of the times she'd caught herself observing him, she felt an odd stirring inside of her. The feeling was entirely new and extremely distracting.

The deep magenta and gray overcast skies opened and poured down acid rain, as flashes of mauve lightning lit everything like daylight. Severe winds ripped through the small valley and threatened to tear the roof from Lyte's den.

She and 51 worked feverishly to repair her home's relay system. A stray lightning bolt had hit the den and caused damage to the system and compromised the power levels to her home. This wouldn't normally be a huge issue, however it was immediately following storms like these, that Zortosk Beasts hunted in large numbers.

With a lack of sufficient power, her perimeter alarms and defenses would be all but useless to ward them off. Generally, they would avoid her altogether because of the auto-defense system, but without it they were apt to breach the perimeter of her den. Manually fighting a pack of Zortosk Beasts wasn't a challenge she'd relish.

"Lyte, I require the replacement relay from the repair kit," 51 said.

As Lyte reached into the kit, she sensed 51's gaze on her. She followed the angle of his stare and realized that he'd been focused on her necklace.

51 cocked his head in curiosity. "What purpose does that medallion serve? May I scan it?"

Lyte reached for the medallion and rubbed it in between her fingers with unconscious thought. She eventually glanced down and held it out on its chain. It had become so much a part of her, that she barely realized she wore it.

"No," she said, with more venom than she intended. "It was given to me by my mother. It's all I have left of her."

Lyte gazed off into space, and continued to caress the medallion. The image of her mother's chartreuse skinned face burned in her mind. Her strong, yet feminine beauty reminded her of the Tarkarian Desert Bloom. A beautiful, vibrant flower which grew in one of the harshest environments on the planet.

Her mother had entrusted the talisman to her with a great sense of urgency and desperation. Lyte couldn't recall ever seeing her mother without it. She'd always thought it nothing more than a sacred family heirloom, but on that day she received it, she knew in her heart it was so much more.

"No, not that one. The other one," 51 said.

Lyte snapped from her reverie uncliped the medallion she found by the pod and handed it to 51.

"This appears to be an outdated halogenic sentry drive," 51 said.

Lyte narrowed her gaze at him. Something about this gave her an eerie sensation. She couldn't quite put her finger on why and hesitated to voice her concern.

"What does it do?" She asked.

51 froze in place for a few seconds, as though he were accessing data archives in his positronic brain. Lyte noted that this motion deviated from the more human actions he had adopted as of late.

"I'm not entirely certain," 51 responded. "My data files on this device's functions have been corrupted. I will have to manually insert it into my UPP."

Lyte looked at him in a curious manner.

He recognized her expression with an almost human nod. "My Universal Processing Port. It's the only way for me to determine whether I can access the data."

51 reached to press the side of his neck and expose a data port. After a brief hesitation, he began to place the drive into his UPP.

A sense of dread surged through Lyte that she could no longer ignore. She dashed towards 51 with an outstretched arm, "Wait! We don't know what that will do to you!"

Her last minute effort to stop him was in vain as he had already inserted the drive into his positronic brain. At first there was no change in

51, then within seconds his entire body seized and he stood rigid, with an inhuman expression on his face. His eyes flash with a brilliant blue light before they shifted to dark orbs with glowing blue circles at their center.

CHAPTER ELEVEN

Lyte took a step back, her body reacted with instinct and tensed in preparation for a confrontation. Despite the fact that she had grown to consider the cyborg an ally and friend, decades of fighting for survival took over.

She unsheathed her blades and slid into a fighting stance with her arms raised in front of her. She narrowed her eyes at 51 and focused on him, waiting for any sign of movement.

He remained still as his eyes flashed with a blue light once more, before the entire room was enveloped in a dim, muted virtual reality hologram.

It took only a brief second for her to recognize the scene and in that instant her heart sank. Bile rose in her throat and she found it difficult to breathe.

"No," she gasped.

A few feet from where she stood, the holographic image of her mother stood. Shock permeated her body as she watched in horror, helpless to change the events of the past and destined to relive that moment in the present.

Lyte saw the Krag warriors converge on her mother. When the warriors came into view and had gotten close enough, Luma fired her weapon. One shot pierced a Krag warrior's chest, while the blast from another sentry was deflected by her energy shield as Luma darted between trees for cover.

Luma managed take out another warrior in her path with a head shot, as a blast bounced off of her shield and took out two more warriors nearby.

Lyte's eyes grew large with a sliver of hope that her mother had somehow survived.

With an animalistic cry, she watched Luma attack the remaining sentries. She had only advanced a few feet when a stray pulse round grazed Luma's right shoulder and caused her to stumble backwards. Another round hit her gauntlet and damaged it.

Her energy shield fizzled and lost power, as another blast from the Krag warrior grazed her in the leg and caused her to fall to the ground.

A churning of bile in Lyte's stomach caused her to retch. She couldn't avert her eyes as she watched her mother struggle to pick herself up off the ground as she continued to fire her weapon at the Krag warriors.

A pulse round hit Luma squarely in the chest, and leaves a gaping hole in its wake. She fell to her knees immobilized, as blood dripped from her mouth.

Luma strained to scream, "Srom Silaropmet!" before she crumpled to the ground.

Lyte witnessed the camera angle of the hologram pan out. It revealed that 51 held the pulse rifle that killed her mother.

The hologram slowly dissolved and Lyte stared at 51 with an incredulous expression. She tried to make sense of what she'd just witnessed. She slowly begans to back away from 51.

"No...it can't be!" Lyte screamed.

51 continued to stand inhumanly still and rigid. His eyes flashed from blue, to glowing red. The change in color gave him a demonic look, which caused Lyte's heart to race even faster.

"You are in direct violation of the Krag Empire, Directive 131345. All sentient lifeforms on this planet are subject to eradication," 51 said.

Tears welled in Lyte's eyes. A swell of anger surged through her and threatened to boil over. Her gaze narrowed and filled with venom. "You killed my mother, my family, my people. Why?"

51 turned his head and gave her an empty gaze, "Because your species is inconsequential and its existence is of no benefit to the Krag Empire."

Blood rushed to Lyte's head and her heart pounded. She gripped her blades and charged at 51. The *Kill Frenzy* consumed her and animalistic instinct took control. A surge of adrenaline augmented her already superbly enhanced strength and reflexes as she thrust her weapons at 51.

His own inhuman reflexes allowed him to easily evade most of her strikes. She managed to slice his arm with one blade and embed the other deep into the center of his chest.

51 reached out with blinding speed, grabbed her by the neck and lifted her off the ground. Lyte struggled to free herself, ignoring the pain as the cyborg crushed her throat, which caused her to drop her blades.

"Your struggles are in vain. Your species is not strong enough to defeat the Krag Empire," 51 said.

In a last ditch effort, Lyte slung her head forward and head-butted 51. The strike had virtually no effect on him and sent insurmountable pain through her head and neck.

51 tossed her several meters across the pasture with almost no effort. Lyte landed in an awkward position and familiar with the pain, knew that she'd broken at least one rib and sprained her wrist. She struggled to regain her breath and maintain consciousness.

51 removed Lyte's blade from his chest as a crackle of energy emitted from the hole left in its wake. He looked curiously at the weapon before he tossed it aside.

He turned to Lyte, who had lunged toward him, having picked up the other weapon with her uninjured hand. She kept her eyes locked with his as she rammed the blade back into his chest. This time, Lyte held onto the weapon and twisted it.

Before she could react, 51 had shot his fist out at her and struck her in the chest. The blow sent her flying into a nearby tree on the edge of the pasture, twenty meters away.

Blood welled in her mouth and the intense pain forced her eyes shut. She ground her teeth and felt herself slipping into unconsciousness. Lyte struggled to breathe and forced herself to remain completely still.

She could feel 51's presence above her. He moved in near her and pressed his fingers along her neck. Lyte rolled to the side and activated her gauntlet's shield as she slammed it against 51's neck. The resulting blow sent his head flying from his shoulders. Sparks flew from his headless body as it seized and spasmed.

Lyte used the last of her strength to push the cyborg's body away from her. She laid back, exhausted and gasping for air. Her head spun and her consciousness was slipping fast. Her ears registered sounds of an aircraft descending near her. She tried to open her eyes, but only caught a glimpse of it before she lost consciousness.

EPILOGUE

Three forms exited the spacecraft and approached Lyte's unconscious body. Dr. Meko darted ahead of the other two and knelt beside the body of the young, green skinned woman. Mac and Liz hung back a couple of meters and kept their eyes on the perimeter.

Dr. Meko used her Emergency Medical Diagnostic Device to scan the woman's body and assess her condition. The handheld device emitted a blue light as Meko hovered it just above her. A series of chirps, hums and pings sounded in a low volume with each movement of Meko's hand.

"Dr. Meko, is she alive?" Liz asked.

The doctor frowned, the furrows in her brow made the unique, red tribal markings on her forehead form a random pattern, "According to the EMDD, her vitals are low, but stable. I need her transported back to the ship and put into the regeneration chamber immediately."

Liz pursed her lips and looked over at Mac. He flashed her his ever-present Machiavellian grin, but his dark brown eyes betrayed the severity of his mood with a grim countenance. She knew that despite his roguish bravado, Mac was intelligent and introspective. He knew what was at stake here, and she had no doubt he was prepared to do whatever was necessary to complete the mission at hand.

A chime from the communicator Liz wore on her belt, snapped her back from her thoughts. She unclipped it and looked at the display, it was Chip. She pressed a button and activated a viewscreen. Chip's clean shaven, cherubic face was twisted into an expression of chaotic anxiety. His mop of tousled dirty blond hair gave him the look of a child.

"Do you really think that's wise? We don't know anything about her species, or this planet," Chip said.

Mac leaned in towards Liz with a perplexed expression. "Again, why did he send us here? Is this woman actually a part of the Submerge experiment?"

Liz frowned. "I don't know. But, I guess we'll find out when she wakes up…if she wakes up."

A group of surrounding shadows appeared to move of their own volition and formed a humanoid mass near where they stood. A being dressed in a black hooded robe stood in the wake of the shadows. Its facial features were hidden behind a silver mask which could barely be seen within the recesses of the hood.

The being seemed to float as it moved towards Liz, Mac and Dr. Meko.

"Figure, what did you learn?" Liz asked.

"I have searched the ruins in the city. There are no indigenous life forms remaining. And there is no sign of the weapon," the Figure said.

The Figure's voice resonated deeply with an eerie, otherworldly tone. His robes flowed with movement, despite the absence of any wind.

"Is it just me, or is he the creepiest thing in the galaxy," Mac whispered in Liz' ear.

She ignored him, but allowed herself a half grin as she turned and stepped towards Dr. Meko and the injured woman. She had been strapped down onto an emergency hover board which slowly floated towards the ship.

"Uhhh, guys! The ship is picking up multiple red dots on the planet surface. This can't be good," Chip said.

Liz pursed her lips. "Can you be more specific? The Figure just said we were all clear."

She watched as Chip worked frantically at the instrument panel in front of him. "I'm sorry. I'm still getting used to the ship's language," Chip said, before he made an audible gasp.

Liz raised an eyebrow, 'What's wrong, is everything okay?"

Chip moved around the console, his hands a blur in the viewscreen, "Guys! The red dots are moving towards the blue dots, which I suppose are you. Get back to the ship now!"

Mac drew his blaster and scanned the perimeter, "Dr. Meko, we've got to get back to the ship, now!"

From the edge of the woods several dozen men, all dressed in gray jumpsuits, emerged. Their expressions were grim and their eyes glowed an eerie red, as did their arms.

"Krag sentries," Mac shouted, as he began to move away from the area.

He held his blaster in front of him and fired a barrage of rounds at them. The figures continued to advance towards them from the surrounding woods.

"Move, we've got to get out of here," Mac said.

Dr. Meko strained to move the hover board which carried the injured woman into the ship, "I need some help here!"

The Figure transported over to Meko and helped her carry the hover board into the ship.

Liz closed her eyes, took a deep breath and opened them. They glowed with a brilliant blue light, as she raised her right hand which crackled with the same vibrant blue light. A pulse of energy shot from her hand and destroyed one of the Krag cyborgs.

"Mac, we need to get back to the ship and lift off this rock now," she said, as she turned and towards the ship.

***

A swirling miasma of color formed near the edge of the woods seconds after the spacecraft pierced the planet's atmosphere. The vortex opened and out stepped a tall, dark skinned warrior.

The muscular warrior scowled as he surveyed the clearing ahead. A young woman named Zeer, stood close behind him.

The area was filled with dozens of men in gray jumpsuits, with glowing red eyes. They focused their attention on Zeer and the warrior.

"Lord Raz, it would appear that this planet has been taken over by the Krag Empire's Sentries," Zeer said.

Raz scowled, "That much is obvious."

One of the cyborg sentries approached them and stopped a couple of meters away.

"Where is she," Raz said, as a field of energy surrounded him.

"You are in violation of the Krag Empire and will be destroyed," the cyborg said, as it charged Raz with inhuman speed.

However, with superior reflexes, Raz shot out his right hand, grabbed the cyborg around its neck and raised him off the ground with herculean strength.

The automaton struggled in his grip before Raz twisted his hand sharply and snapped its neck. Sparks flew from its head, smoke swirled from its ears and mouth, and the eyes which once had been filled with brilliant red light, faded to darkness.

The other cyborgs converged upon them in unified fury.

Zeer produced an energy bow and stood back to back with Raz. She fired a barrage of explosive shafts at the cyborgs.

"I will find Liz, the daughter of Ni're, and nothing and no one will stop me!" Raz spat.

An intense field of energy surrounded him as a miasma of colored light. Large arcs of power crackled in the heated air, as he tensed his powerful body and bellowed with a mighty roar.

***

Liz, Mac and Dr. Meko stood together in the observation deck of the ship. The young woman laid on a table in a stasis field. They stood motionless as they witnessed a huge mushroom cloud erupt from the area of the planet where they had left.

A sudden chill ran along the spine of Liz. Somehow, she knew that the explosion they had seen, foreshadowed dangers yet to come. She wrapped her arms around herself, turned and walked away.

GALLERY

SUBMERGE
ECHO 51

©2016

132

ABOUT THE AUTHOR

John F. Allen is the author of numerous novels and short stories. His first full length novel, The God Killers, was published in 2013 by Seventh Star Press. Several of his short stories have been published by various publishers over the course of the past five years.

His official website is: www.johnfallenwriter.com

ACKNOWLEDGMENTS

I want to thank my editor, Linda Sullivan for her hard work and dedication to this novelization project.

In addition, I would like to take this opportunity to thank Demetrius Witherspoon for selecting me to pen the novelization of his cinematic creation. I am truly honored and humbled to be a part of this amazing franchise and I look forward to its continued success in the future.

AUTOGRAPHS

Made in the USA
Monee, IL
03 May 2023

32771687R10079